Dear Parent:
Your child's love of reading starts here!

Every child learns to read in a different way and at his or her own speed. Some go back and forth between reading levels and read favorite books again and again. Others read through each level in order. You can help your young reader improve and become more confident by encouraging his or her own interests and abilities. From books your child reads with you to the first books he or she reads alone, there are I Can Read Books for every stage of reading:

SHARED READING
Basic language, word repetition, and whimsical illustrations, ideal for sharing with your emergent reader

BEGINNING READING
Short sentences, familiar words, and simple concepts for children eager to read on their own

READING WITH HELP
Engaging stories, longer sentences, and language play for developing readers

READING ALONE
Complex plots, challenging vocabulary, and high-interest topics for the independent reader

ADVANCED READING
Short paragraphs, chapters, and exciting themes for the perfect bridge to chapter books

I Can Read Books have introduced children to the joy of reading since 1957. Featuring award-winning authors and illustrators and a fabulous cast of beloved characters, I Can Read Books set the standard for beginning readers.

A lifetime of discovery begins with the magical words "I Can Read!"

Visit www.icanread.com for information
on enriching your child's reading experience.

Library of Congress catalog card number: 2011941959
ISBN 978-0-06-207484-3 (trade bdg.)—ISBN 978-0-06-207483-6 (pbk.)

      12 13 14 15 16   SCP   10 9 8 7 6 5 4 3 2 1 ❖   First Edition

Marley

FIREHOUSE DOG

**BASED ON THE BESTSELLING BOOKS BY
JOHN GROGAN**

COVER ILLUSTRATION BY RICHARD COWDREY

TEXT BY CAITLIN BIRCH

INTERIOR ILLUSTRATIONS BY LYDIA HALVERSON

HARPER
An Imprint of HarperCollinsPublishers

One fine day,

Marley and his family went for a walk.

They went past the firehouse.

"Hello there," said the fire chief.

"Today is our open house.

Would you like a tour?"

OPEN
HOUSE

"We'd love a tour!" said Mommy.

"You stay here, Marley,

and don't get into trouble,"

said Daddy.

Cassie tied Marley up.

The family followed the chief inside.

But Marley wanted to go, too.

He started to chew on his leash.

The chief showed the family

all over the firehouse.

They saw the kitchen, the day room,

the sleeping room, and the classroom.

"See, Cassie?" said the chief.

"Even my firefighters go to school.

This is where they learn

to be ready for any emergency."

Marley finished chewing

through his leash.

"Good job," Marley thought.

Then he started his own tour.

Marley saw what was cooking

in the kitchen.

He tried out the chairs in the day room.

Marley rested in the sleeping room.

Marley took a look

at the classroom lessons.

"Now I'll show you the garage,"
said the chief.

He led the family back through
the rooms of the firehouse.

Oh, no!

Every room was a mess!

"Which one of my firefighters
did this?" asked the chief.
"We'd better see what is going on
in the garage," he said.

"My hoses!"

cried the chief.

"What is the meaning of this?"

"I think we know the meaning of this

all too well, chief," said Daddy.

Just then, Marley tripped on a hose.

He fell into some gear.

Cassie saw the gear

on the floor begin to move.

"Chief!" Cassie called.

"Emergency!"

Suddenly Marley popped up!

"Chief, meet Marley,

your messy firefighter," Daddy said.

"Chief, we are very sorry,"

said Mommy.

"It's all right,"

said the chief, smiling.

"We're used to emergencies."

"With a dog like Marley,
we're used to emergencies, too,"
said Daddy.

Marley and the family helped clean up
all the rooms of the firehouse.

When they were done,

the chief had a surprise for Marley.

"Marley, you can be our mascot anytime," said the chief.

FIREDOG
for a day